ALOISIUS
ALOISIUS
ALOISIUS
ALOISIUS

AN ANGEL FROM MUNICH

A Story by Ludwig Thoma

As Told by Adolf Gondrell

A Book Version of the Moving Picture

Created by Gertraud and Walter Reiner

Edited and Introduced

by

W. F. Karlos

W. Ludwig Verlag

Art Work: Gertraud and Walter Reiner
Original Title: Ein Münchner im Himmel
English Version: Edith Dyckerhoff and Matthias Büttner

Third Edition 1997

ISBN 3-7757-3462-8

Manufactured by Gorenjski Tisk, Kranj (Slovenia)
The original story by Ludwig Thoma in the version of Adolf Gondrell is published in this book permission of the R. Piper & Co. Verlag in Munich, Germany, possessor of all rights for the works of Ludwig Thoma.

This is Alois Hingerl . . .

and actually this foreword should have been written in the language he speaks: in Bavarian. But that is unfortunately impossible. Because Bavarian is a dialect of the German language not even always understood by other Germans! (And at times the Bavarians are quite proud of this.) It is spoken around the snow capped mountains of the Bavarian Alps, in the villages and towns of Southern Germany, and of course in Munich, the capital of Bavaria. It is a very picturesque language, which is able to express feelings and opinions in a way no other language can. (This is at least what the Bavarians like to think.) But part of it seems to be understood everywhere—even in heaven!

Because Alois Hingerl is the former name of Angel Aloisius, whom you see gliding down to earth in the upper right hand corner of this page. And how this typical Bavarian came to be an angel, and what happened to him in heaven, is told in this colourful little book. Millions of people already enjoyed the adventures of Angel Aloisius in the delightful cartoon film and watched him getting involved—really without any fault of his own—in the fate of the Bavarian Government.

Some outsiders, non-Bavarians of course, have suggested that it might have been better to prevent Alois Hingerl's appearance in public in order to save the reputation of the Bavarians. But why? Ever since the famous Bavarian writer and poet Ludwig Thoma wrote the original story and ever since the unforgettable folk-actor Adolf Gondrell recited it in his own version to thousands of delighted listeners, the grumbling little Bavarian railway porter Alois Hingerl has been making more and more friends everywhere, and they all like him.

And to give even more people around the world the chance to meet him is the purpose of this book. It is based on the prize-winning cartoon film by Gertraud and Walter Reiner, who are both dyed-in-the-wool Bavarians and caught the atmosphere of Munich in a way nobody else could. And we hope that the adventures of Angel Aloisius will be enjoyed by everybody—by people who have visited Bavaria, by people who plan to visit Bavaria, and perhaps even by people who never heard of this fabulous country!
In order to give non-Bavarians a chance to understand some of the more complicated dialect expressions, the publisher has included a short glossary at the end of the book.

W. F. Karlos.

In Memory of

Ludwig Thoma,

the Outstanding, Old-Bavarian Poet

and his

Interpreter

Adolf Gondrell

Alois Hingerl, porter No, 172 at Munich Central Station

HB
HB
Dienstmann
172

2
3

worked so energetically one day

that he just dropped dead.

RAUCHER
3
172

·Dienstmann·
172

Two little angels carried him to heaven with some difficulty
where Saint Peter welcomed him

and told him

that from now on his name would be Angel Aloisius.

·ALOI

He presented him with a harp
and informed him of the heavenly house rules. "…from eight in the morning until twelve noon," he said, "you will jubilate, and from twelve noon until eight in the evening you will sing 'Hosannah'!"

“Wos is?„ asked Aloisius.

"…from eight in the morning until twelve noon: jubilating.
And from twelve noon until eight in the evening: singing 'Hosannah'!"

“So – hmhm – ja, and when do I get something z’trinka”?
“You will get your Manna in due time”
said Saint Peter slightly annoyed, and left him.

“A u w e h ! „ grumbled Angel Aloisius, “that is going to be s c h ö f a d!
I should jubilate from eight to twelve…
and I thought there was no work in heaven.”

But, he finally sat down on a cloud and began to sing as he was told, "Hallelujah! Hallelujah!!"

A very high-spirited intellectual angel came gliding by.

“Hey! You!” called Aloisius, “how about some Schmaizla, a Pris?
Geh weida let’s have some!”
But the intellectual angel was revolted by this vulgar idea.
He just whispered “Hosannah” and departed.

Aloisius became furious: “Ja – what kind of a damischer Depp is this?” he shouted, “if you don’t have any Schmaizla you just dont, right? A man can expect a decent answer, can’t he? You gscherte Ruab’n, you! Mei Liaber, what people they have up here! A – A – what did I get into!”
And once more he sat down on his cloud
and continued to jubilate

SIUS.

– but his anger showed in his singing

and he was shouting so loudly that the Heavenly Father next door
awoke from His afternoon nap and asked with astonishment:
"From whence cometh this noise?"

ALOISIUS

At once He sent for Saint Peter, who came running,
and together they heard the scandalous jubilating of Angel Aloisius:
"Hallelujah --- Sacklzementhallelujah! Hallelujah!"
Saint Peter hurried away and dragged Aloisius before the Lord.

The Heavenly Father looked at him a long time and then He spoke: "Oh, I see – – – an Angel from Munich! That's what I thought! Now tell me – – – what is all this shouting about?"

That was exactly what Aloisius had been waiting for.
He was so furious that he started right out:
“I don’t like all these things!”
“I don’t like to have wings!!”

ALOISIUS

“I don’t like to sing Hosannah!!”
“I don’t like to drink Manna”
“Instead of beer!”

“And let me make clear:
“I do not like to sing!!!”

"Saint Peter," said the Lord, "this will never do! But I have an idea: We shall employ him as messenger conveying Our heavenly advice to the Bavarian Government. So he can fly to Munich once or twice a week – and his good soul will 'Rest in Peace'!"

An die Bayerische Staatsregierung

When Aloisius heard this, he felt very happy indeed!
Soon he got his first delivery job – a letter

– and flew down to earth.

HB

And when once again he felt the soil of Munich
under his feet,
it seemed to him, that now he was really in heaven.
And following his old habits
he immediately went to the Hofbräuhaus

and found his accustomed place empty and waiting for him.

Dienstm

And good old Kathi, the waitress, was still there

And he ordered a Mass of beer

HB
HB
HB
HB

And another Mass

And he forgot his letter and his job
And ordered another Mass, and another, and still another one…

and he just sat and is still sitting there today.

Dienstmann

And that's the reason
the Bavarian Government to this day,

has to do without Divine suggestions.

Dienstmann

Glossary

Bavarian dialect expressions which cannot be translated even into German.

Wos is?:	What? What's going on?
z'trinka:	Something to drink.
auweh!:	Woe is me!
schö fad:	quite boring, unpleasant.
Schmaizla:	actually Schmalzler: snuff tobacco, an old tradition that is still kept up in Bavaria.
Pris:	a pinch of snuff tobacco.
geh weida:	come on now!
damischer Depp:	a silly daft person.
g'scherte Ruab'n:	literally, a rube with a homemade haircut, a country bumpkin, a stupid person.
mei Liaber:	oh! my dear!
Sacklzementhallelujah:	a mild swear word, euphemism for "Sacramento!" literally, a sack of cement.
Hofbräuhaus:	the famous Munich brewery and beer hall once owned by the royal house of Bavaria. Hof: court.
Mass:	a "measure" of beer consisting of 1 liter, the size of the traditional beer stein.

ALOISIUS
ALOISIUS
ALOISIUS